# Love in the Sudan
# & other stories

Eric Mugambi

ISBN: 978-9966-804-29-7

# DEDICATION

To Edna and Moira
My Sun and my Moon

These stories span more than a decade.
I hope you will enjoy them.
Eric Mugambi

# CONTENTS

Why we write

We write to learn, to have fun, to create
We write to thrill, to heal, to ignite
But mostly, we just write

# ACKNOWLEDGMENTS

To those without whom the characters in this book,
would never have come to life

# FIRST LOVE

Who was your first Love? How did you meet? What was the most attractive thing about them? Where was your first date? What was that song you hummed on your way home from that 'not-so secret' rendezvous? Was it 'Careless whispers', as it was for me? Whatever fates conspired our paths must cross, I cannot tell, but Megan was simply irresistible! It was the closest I would ever get to love at first sight. In my mind's eye, she was always beautiful. Was it the way she smiled conspiratorially, in my direction, during those long boring afternoon classes? Or was it the encouraging sparkle in her eyes, when I rose to contribute the least trivial of remarks, no doubt motivated by some inconsolable craving for her attention? Was it the angle her fragile chin tipped, almost in shyness, whenever our eyes locked, in brief moments of sheepishness? Was it how effortlessly our cares drifted away as we held hands and her head rested upon my shoulder on the drive back from the random day trip? I wish it were that simple, but nothing ever is. Megan and I were not to last, for we soon went our different ways. Nature in its eternal wisdom decreed that Megan proceed to the US and that I become a doctor. Slowly, yet inevitably, the space between us grew into an impenetrable chasm burying with it our youthful dreams and aspirations. You cannot imagine my surprise then, when she came back into my life after a 16 year long hiatus. It all started through a request for friendship from a mutual acquaintance, who after a series of exchanges on Facebook Chat, threw in an unsubtle hint about Megan and the name she went by on Facebook. As I clicked 'discreetly' on Megan's profile, I was 'busted' by the delightful faces of two little children, smiling from the cover picture, who instantly reflected back the smiling eyes, the impeccable nose, and the dimpled cheeks of that goddess from my past. On one of the profile photos, she came to life. Unmistakably her, despite the softened features of motherhood, and the barrel chested hunk, that held her in an intimate embrace, yet still managed to flash a perfect set of white teeth at the camera. Other albums bore names such as Baby's christening, Trip to Sea world, IOS, Blessing and Dallas. Having exceeded what I deemed a decent interval, from a user with very limited guest rights, I stared at the screen to observe my pointer hover on top of the 'Friend request' tab for a while, before reluctantly moving on to the tab ushering me back into the frenzy of World Cup 2014. If you choose to believe that we are living across different dimensions of time, simultaneously, then you will see Megan and I holding hands in that parallel universe at 18, dancing our cares away under the blue light of the moon. If you choose to consign such belief to the Sci-fi corner of your local library, then you will no doubt be moved by the unparalleled power of the human memory - that unique and cavernous repository where Megan remains eternally irresistible.

I wish it were that simple, but nothing ever is.

# THE PIANIST

The show opened to a full house. It would later be reported that more tickets had been sold than were seats in the fabled theatre. It would escape mention that this was the Maestro's last appearance in concert. The young prodigy sat by the illuminated Steinway, on a taciturn stage that felt out of place. The deafening applause that reverberated across the hall ebbed away nonchalantly as he took time to adjust his music score. He felt the familiar lightness in his head, the heightened awareness of his heartbeat and the increasing impediment down his throat, sensations that even he would never grow accustomed to. Yet, he took it all in stride, lifting his eyes across the inscrutable forms inhabiting the darkened auditorium, until the entire concert hall was transformed into the image of an artist's canvas. He allowed himself to transcend to a higher plane where he, the artist, stood poised to forge a lasting impression, perhaps even a masterpiece, onto this vulnerable canvas. Yet, today was different. Slowly and synchronous with his measured breaths, the maze of jumbled dots on the piano rack slid into focus and the endless rows of notes and annotations registered in his alert sensorium. He was ready. His fingers pressed lightly on the ivory notes. Somewhere, tucked away and unseen, levers twitched, hammers stirred, strings shuddered and the most wonderful sound rent across the hall. The melody flirted surreptitiously in and out of the labyrinth of chords that fashioned the harmony so that the audience was transported out of the concert hall and onto the virtual canvas over which the pianist lorded, not unlike a medieval aristocrat over a rabble of peasants. The music played, full and sonorous, vivid yet distant. And it seemed that the pianist caused a note to be suspended in the air, long enough for the effect to be palpable, before snapping it out of the range of his audience, and back to the next round of notes emanating from the dimly lit stage. It was the unmistakable sound of love. And it betrayed that tonight, the pianist was in love. Sloshes of crimson red fell upon the imaginary canvas as the story was told. Gentler strokes of brush, conjured the object of his affection, so that the audience reclining upon the edges of the canvas beheld her delicate features and her quiet poise. And as the music infused life onto the virtual canvas, the audience sat enwrapped in the spell of the pianist's genius. A random act of kindness and a chance meeting had decreed that their paths should cross. He could tell from the moment he saw her that she would haunt his memory for as long as he lived. He accepted that they would never be together. Out on the fringes of the canvas, real faces concealed in the darkened auditorium, the audience sensed that the tone was changing. Heavy blots of grey descended upon the artist's pad. The music switched to a minor scale. The pianist's right foot pressed lightly upon the pedal, so that the strings were stifled, and their sound restrained. Out on the illuminated stage, the pianist's hands could be observed in a flurry of activity. Scales transitioned flawlessly beneath the deft fingers, so that the audience was drenched in the sound of unrequited love. On the artist's canvas, the masterpiece neared completion, an iridescent orange sky at sunset, against which two silhouettes held hands in a wistful manner, peering towards a fickle horizon. The girl that had walked into the concert hall, well into the performance, stood transfixed by one of the pillars at the threshold. Her features were delicate, her poise quiet. In the darkness, the tears in her downcast eyes went unnoticed. She could not tell what force had driven her here tonight, into this concert hall. Yet, as part of her contemplated instant flight, the other willed for the music not to stop. And as the pianist's rendition culminated into a standing ovation with the curtain closing upon the dazzling performance, she knew for sure what she had known all along. And the pianist had made it all possible. It was the reason she would wait for him. That he would come, she was certain. For the darling girl he had played about was her. The story of the world renowned pianist that had played for love generated considerable sentiment. Charities wrote to express their gratitude for funds donated from the proceeds of the concerts. Local women blubbered endlessly about the love struck lad that had wooed them with the music - fifteen straight months. That he had pledged not to stop until his affections were reciprocated did not go down well with the swig of frothy beer at the local male dominated pub. Speculation remained rife about the identity of the woman on the imaginary canvas, she that had finally put an end to all the music. Some said she was tall and dark. Others said she was short and bright.

An anonymous caller on the favorite radio station described her as delicate with a quiet poise.

# THE FEELING

The Feeling had become a fact of his existence. He could not really describe it as much as he remained all too aware of its pervasive presence. The Feeling bore no colour but it did remind him of the hue of night or that of outer space. It subdued him completely, devastated him for days on end. On the days the Feeling lifted, he would be reincarnated; he would feel astir and his heart would lighten. On one such day, he had met her. He first saw the colours, genial, enchanting and hypnotizing. 'I couldn't agree more,' he had replied to her remark about the weather, 'beautiful day to be outside. But I guess we are destined to watch from this side of the window.' She had smiled, a subtle beguiling smile, so that her colour revealed its different shades, and his heart was enamoured with warmth. She was easy to talk to, or more to the point, stare at with wonderment, as her voice weaved in and out of the cacophony of voices buffeting them. And even long after the sessions stood dismissed for the day, they would lag behind everyone else, talking about nothing, and everything. At the end of the conference, amid the frenzy of delegates scampering out of meeting rooms, they had said their farewells. The colours were soft and fickle. He prepared for their rendezvous with meticulous flourish. His visit to a startled barber rid him of the unsightly mane. He then proceeded to his local draper and was outfitted with a stylish suit. A fashionable pair of loafers awaited collection at the high end mall. 'Must not overdo it,' he thought to himself, even as he spent considerable time selecting the right fragrance and the choicest of flowers – blended to complement her colours. And then, without so much as knocking, the Feeling returned. And he felt powerless as he drifted back, almost nostalgically, into its familiar tenacious hold. Somewhere in the real world, inside the most sought after restaurant in town, a dainty girl sat at a candle lit table for two. An untouched glass of sauvignon Blanc stood gauntly at half arm's reach. 'Courtesy of your dinner companion,' the sommelier intoned, pouring out from a frosted pampered bottle. Across the street, the gentleman dressed-for-dinner stood transfixed, where the Feeling had gripped him. Peering through the haze that had descended upon his field of vision, he could barely make out her silhouette through the restaurant's dimmed windows. And yet the Feeling, had allowed its captive one saving grace; for in the flickering candle light, her shades of crimson were unmistakable, and for no particular reason, that infinitesimal detail gave him a modicum of peace. It was some time before he turned away, and walked ungainly into the night.

There were no colours – only darkness.

# LOVE IN THE SUDAN

He had come to this place in search of himself, and then he had found her. The flight to Loki had been on board an East African Air jet engine craft at an altitude of twenty thousand feet. From Loki they had boarded a small double propeller Dornier to Marial Lou. She sat next to him. He saw that she was pretty, even beautiful at close range. He wondered what had brought her out into this place, into this wilderness, yet he dared not ask. He had come here for the solitude and the tranquility, and he did not feel any desire to explain his reasons to anyone. He had left a letter for them back home. Not that it said much. Just so they should not worry about him. Perhaps she too was in search of something much dearer. He felt no compelling desire to find out her reasons. The gaunt spindly man that had travelled with them was an Italian of good cheer. He had worked for the Organisation in many parts of the world riddled with famine and war, and often told of his escapades in a comical accent that always began with the drawn out word *'Ima...r....gine.'* As the plane circled overhead preparing to land on the rugged weather beaten runway, he had caught a glimpse of the hospital and the compound. The airstrip was littered with hoardes of excited men, women and children alike, as if the landing of an aircraft had become indelibly entrenched into the calendar of events of the Marial Lou community - this despite the fact that the plane made the landing every two weeks. A few stray dogs crisscrossed the runway and one felt trepidation that a collision with a plane was inevitable. At the welcoming dinner that night, he learned her name was Hazel. She spoke with a sweet voice and a quiet assurance and he sat hanging upon every word that came out of her full scarlet lips. He had then retired to his leaning *Tukul,* too tired to indulge in a much needed shower, yet his mind remained unsettled with the relentless intrusion of her sweet voice into the very fabric of his dreams. His days started early so that he would be done with the demanding work way ahead of the midday sun. The nights, he spent tucked away inside his crumpled *Tukul* catching up with his Dinka vocabulary. And then when he went to sleep he would think about her. He would listen to her voice deep in his thoughts and the feeling would lull him into a deep slumber. But all that was before he met the talkative, flamboyant character that went by the call sign 'Charlie Mike'. One long boring evening, they had donned their mud boots and overcoats and crept quietly out of the compound. He had plodded heavily behind Charlie Mike up the muddy path winding into the darkness. The journey had ended abruptly outside a nondescript looking *Tukul* from which emanated the intense cacophony of cheerful, happy voices. '*Chibak*' a loud voice ushered them into the dimly lit room. Around a small dusty stool, sat a medley of stooped figures wielding small untidy tumblers within trembling grips. '*Lima India*,' Charlie Mike who seemed a regular here whispered the name of the drink·to him. Without further ado, two dirty mugs were placed in front of them. A malodorous clear liquid was carefully sieved into the cups. After a hearty toast in his honour, Charlie Mike and he had raised the cups to their mouths. It was a little past midnight as they made their lonely journey home. Bidding '*wabaiyoo nyak*' to Charlie Mike, he had staggered back into his *Tukul*. Try as he would, the once repressed feelings for the girl with the sweet voice surged to the surface. Was it why he had come to this place? His legs carried him out into the night and in the direction of her *Tukul*. Her lights were out, he saw. No doubt she was asleep. Resolving to let her know once and for all how much he adored her, he took in a deep breath and held out his knuckles to impart a knock onto her door, but suddenly his knees buckled and he felt his courage ebb away. He crawled back into his *Tukul*, a defeated but also a changed man.

'Dear Hazel,' he wrote.

'I have never been good with words and it could be said of me that I am a man of few words, so pardon me if what I write makes little if any sense to you. Do not think me impolite or presumptuous and should you find this most regrettable intrusion into your space offensive, please do not hesitate to let me know. It is just that I can't seem to get you out of my head. Ever since that very first day by the evening fire it seems that a spell was cast upon my very being. Would you consider meeting me? We could sneak out some wine from the kitchen *Tukul* and gaze at the full moon together; and then maybe we could talk. Tomorrow nine would be fine.

A secret admirer.'

The next morning before setting out to work he called the Dinka girl that worked in the compound and gave the letter to drop by Hazel's *Tukul*. The tall dark girl nodded and smiled conspiratorially. He worked with a vengeance in an attempt to suppress the anxiety seething forth from his very core. Had she read his letter and would she think him imprudent and hasty? Did she ever notice him? Or was it the *Lima India* that had filled him with such grandiose ideas? That evening, the Italian was regaling them with one of his favorite stories… *'Ima…r….gine…,'* but all he could think of was the nine o`clock rendezvous. He was there well before nine, unable to mask his anticipation. The kitchen area was deserted, much to his relief. He moved to the shadows where he felt less exposed and waited for Hazel. But she did not come. That night in his *Tukul*, he wrote:

'Dear Hazel, I did not see you today as arranged and I take it you were not interested in the ravings of a man who has allowed foolish ideas of romance to flourish in his idle mind. Have no fear. I shall trouble you no longer. I just wanted you to know that I came out here in search of something even I myself did not know. I realise now that it was to search for someone dear. Someone I lost touch with a long time ago. Seeing you invoked feelings I had long thought forever gone. For that I shall always be grateful… A friend.'

The next morning before setting out to work he called the Dinka girl that worked in the compound and gave the letter to drop by Hazel's *Tukul*. The girl nodded and smiled. He finished his day early, yet the memory of the beautiful girl by the fire lingered. He hoped things had turned out differently. That she would have noticed him, maybe even liked him. But he remained grateful that she had brought the much-needed jolt into his life. He still felt the irresistible urge to write her once more, just to say goodbye and wish her success with her own journey. That night, he declined the offer from Charlie Mike to accompany him to the *Tukul* with the dirty mugs, where they served the *Lima India*, and sat by the desk lamp in his *Tukul*.

'Dear Hazel,' he wrote, 'the good Italian has confirmed that the plane from Marial Lou departs tomorrow morning. Having come to the end of my pilgrimage, I now feel ready to go back home to my life. I mentioned in the last letter the search that brought me out here and that it was for someone I lost touch with a long time ago. That someone is the man I once was. You might have found me dull, and maybe a bore. Yet once not so long ago, I was alive, full of laughter, and capable of loving. Then one day, something happened that robbed me of all that. I will not bore you with details of my tragedy; just that seeing you stirred back memories long locked up in the back of my mind. I am now ready to confront my past and move on, and learn to live again. Thank you for being the flame that set alight the dying embers of my life… Affectionately yours.'

Hazel woke up earlier than usual the next morning, a thin aura of melancholy encircling. She had heard that the plane from Marial Lou would depart that morning, and that its lone passenger would be the tall quiet man who had kept to himself all during his two-month sojourn. He seemed a decent man but too hardworking, she thought. Yet, she had felt a connection, every time she bumped into him along the compound, and he would avert his gaze and move on, more like a frightened child. And yet she felt a stirring, deep in her heart. They had sat together on the flight to Marial Lou and aside from a few pleasantries, no words had transpired. Yet, her heart bled to find out why he had come out here, into the wild, and why he wore that forlorn look. She had noticed the change in him over the next couple of weeks. All too suddenly, it was as if a veil had lifted off his face, his shoulders relieved of some unseen weight. He wore a smile and even returned her gaze. Yet, he still never uttered a word. And now she was sad to see him leave – strange, since she never really knew him. She waved absent-mindedly along with Charlie Mike, the Italian and the others, as the car ferrying its lone tall passenger to the airstrip disappeared into a long trail of dust down the dirt-laden road. She had just retired to her *Tukul* when a rasp knock rattled the door. Outside, stood a tall Dinka girl. Hazel knew her to be the girl that worked in the compound. In her hand, the girl held out three crumbled envelopes. 'For me?' she asked in well-articulated Dinka. The girl nodded in the affirmative and left. Hazel sat on the unmade bed, sifted through the envelopes, and unwrapped the first letter.

'Dear Hazel, I have never been good with words… pardon me if what I write makes little if any sense to you…,' She read on, a tear forming at the edges of her soft brown eyes.

'Dear Hazel,' the second letter began, 'I take it that you were not interested in the ravings of a man who has allowed foolish ideas of romance to flourish in his idle mind. I shall trouble you no longer… I came out here in search of something… I realise now that it was to search for someone dear… Seeing you, invoked feelings that I had long thought forever gone…,'

Tears now welled up her eyes as she ripped open the third envelope. 'Dear Hazel, the good Italian has confirmed that the plane from Marial Lou departs tomorrow morning… I now feel ready to go back home to my life… You might have found me dull, maybe a bore, but once, not so long ago, I was alive, full of laughter, and capable of loving… I will not bore you with details of my tragedy… Seeing you stirred up memories long locked up in the back of my mind. I am now ready to confront my past… Thank you for being the flame that set alight the dying embers of my life…'

She now sobbed uncontrollably. If only she'd known. In wild desperation, she ran out of her *Tukul* into the garage. The Landcruiser's engine was revving and the driver was sorting out some luggage for transit to Akop. Without hesitation, Hazel jumped into the driver's seat, shifted the gear stick and floored the accelerator. She had to get to him in time. To tell him that she never received the letters till that very moment. And that she too grappled with the same emotions he so eloquently expressed in his letters, that he need not be ashamed. From a distance, she saw the plane taxi on the runway. She drove faster, hooting repeatedly. At the edge of the airstrip the curious bunch of onlookers watched the spectacle, as the Toyota sped along the runway inching closer and closer to the departing plane.

But soon the plane garnered speed, and they watched as its large bulk was hoisted off the ground, and its tail-lights flickered in the afternoon sand storm, ferrying its sole passenger into the horizon.

# MONDAY MORNING

I am not a morning person and I do not believe in Mondays. The memory of a morning, brimming with expectation, rings clear as a bell, when Kaari Mueni, a beguiling specimen of the fairer sex, whose marks in class did not quite live up to her looks, chaperoned me to a secluded spot behind the tuition block for a private viewing of the artwork beneath her school blouse. One can only attribute my fainting episode shortly after to the fact that it was a Monday and a morning! When I came to, it was the buttons on my shirt and not hers, that had been loosened and a petrified Kaari Mueni peered with apprehension from behind a horde of first responders. Someone had placed a concrete block beneath my feet and its razor sharp edge pressed indignantly against my ankles. Kaari Mueni did not repeat her 'breath-taking' feat as she was soon to depart, when her father took up a job on another continent. She left on the chilly morning right after Assembly. It could only have been a Monday because someone had just handed out the weekly meal tickets and Mr. Kogi smelled like the bottles in Miss Ravani's laboratory, no doubt having spent the weekend at the local Shebeen. 'Good morning children,' Mr. Kogi commenced his address after we had belted out the National Anthem in a manner that would have exceedingly delighted the spirits of the founding Fathers. 'Good morning Sir,' we croaked back in unison. 'Thank you children!' the rancid breath doused us from the rostrum, as the source peered down and embarked on a speech that would last the better part of the morning. An hour later, as we filed into our respective classes, I could not help but notice the wily Walter Obiero sneak out of line and proceed to escort Kaari Mueni to a waiting car. My heart simply bled but there was not to be a repeat spectacle of the fateful morning, when the air had brimmed with much expectation. 'Did you borrow my eraser?' enquired a tremulous voice from behind. I turned around to find Japheth Kioko's elliptical face peering from one side of his open desk lid. Before I could respond, the door creaked open with considerable effort, and a small rounded figure stood etched against the petulant rays radiating from the morning sun. The science tutor was covered from head to toe in a white Sari, out of which poked a demure face and a delicate pair of hands. Her entry went unheeded among a band of bickering backbenchers huddled around a game of checkers. On one side of the game-board, sat Willychus Kabetu, a large intense youth with an oily face that was interrupted by numerous pimples. He wore a pained expression, betraying the fact that he was about to lose the third game in a row. 'Nifty Nick' as was his nickname sat on the other side, a crooked grin planted upon his aquiline face. He was a nimble character, with a penchant for relieving small items of worth from unsuspecting benefactors. Smooth talking and evasive, his fingers were reputed to be faster than most people's eyes. That he had never been caught in the act was testimony to his prowess. The spotlight had briefly focused on him once when Mr. Kogi conducted an impromptu inspection of our locked desks, to reveal a trove of geometric sets, missing library books, assorted paraphernalia, and even a pipette, amongst Nick's possessions. But it was the stash of letters neatly fastened with a red ribbon that attracted the headmaster's undivided attention! It was not immediately clear why anyone would pinch love letters, but Jedan Kamau, the aspiring sleuth, suggested during a lunch break that one controlling such information would be in a position to call in any number of favors. The scandal lasted us the better part of the term and took the intervention of the PTA and a generous offering of sore derrières to defuse. I remember the day Nick's father made an appearance and we looked up from our game of football at the dapper looking man in military regalia. In no less articulate fingers than Nifty's, he held one of those carry-bags from the Armed forces liquor store and this was by all appearances a visit to appease Mr. Kogi. Few of us survived the scandal, and Kaari Mueni never forgave me for not writing her a love letter.

'Quiet please,' Miss Ravani pleaded and Willychus was quick to see a way out of the present stalemate. Rising awkwardly from his seat and toppling the game-board with much gusto, he barked out Miss Ravani's appeal in a stern voice that garnered instant compliance from the rest of the class, and deep consternation from Nifty Nick's adherents. 'Good morning class,' Miss Ravani began, 'First *vee* mark vomework.' There was a flurry of activity as we retrieved our workbooks. Behind me, Kioko's desk mate was emphatic that he had not seen his school bag. Miss Ravani started pacing between the rows of neatly placed desks, inspecting our handiwork. She turned abruptly somewhere in the middle of the class and strode back to the front, eliciting sighs of relief from the back bench.

'Exchange *vomework*,' Miss Ravani directed as she wrote the first question on the board, and read it out aloud, '*Vot* is hard *voter?*' The first hand up was Obiero's. 'Hard water is ice, madam,' he replied jokily. A round of giggles emanated from his neighbors much to Miss Ravani's dismay. 'No,' she nodded frantically, '*Zat* is not correct answer *Volter!*' Only when the class appeared stuck on a particularly tough question did Miss Ravani's attention shift to the back benchers, who seemed to require some coercion, beyond school fees, to participate in the class. '*Nicholos,*' she called out, pointing at Nifty, who might very well have been balancing the books of his criminal enterprises. 'Please repeat the question madam,' Nifty Nick responded in an uncharacteristically respectful tone. '*Vot* is *zee* name of an exploding star near *zee* end of its life?' screeched Miss Ravani. We all turned to look at Nifty, whose face remained inscrutable. 'A supernova, madam,' he answered without hesitation. '*Vell* done *Nicholos! Vely vely voll* done!' Miss Ravani's face lit up in a red flush, oblivious to our blank expressions. Nifty even managed a smile, but it was evident he was all too keen to return to his balance sheet. Somewhere outside, the peal of bells could be heard, signaling the end of the first lesson. '*Volter Obilo*,' Miss Ravani summoned the aspiring Comic, 'Collect *voooooooll* books to *zee* teacher's office!' she directed, and paused to monitor Obiero's progress round the class.

Willychus appeared grossly alarmed and behind me, Kioko resumed the futile search for his workbook - so that by 10 o'clock on a cold, unfeeling, Monday morning, Mr. Kogi's punishment list was growing in earnest.

# BILLY THE KID

'They are coming our way!' Joe shouted, his heavy breathing smothering the words. Ahead of us, the ground lay bare, with no hiding place in sight. It would only be moments before Billy and his gang were upon us!

But wait! Where are my manners? It is only fair that I start from the beginning.

Billy the Kid had been incarcerated for two and a half months by the time his notoriety caught my attention. He was head and shoulders above the rest of his crew and spent lots of time in the exercise yard. He maintained an unkempt goatee, a trademark of sorts, which seemed to preserve his revered status amongst his yard mates. 'That's him all right,' Joe tilted his head ever so slightly in the direction of the condemned, 'he's not going to get out of here alive. I wouldn't look in his direction if I were you,' he warned, 'unless you do not mind a nice head butting!' As had become our habit, we had taken to running around the yard for an hour at the least, and as I stole a glance across, I could see Billy and his cronies milling around the makeshift outdoor gym. 'Word has it that several guards rubbed him the wrong way,' Joe continued, 'a mistake that cost them dearly!' 'How long does he have?' I asked as we came round the bend to record our first mile. 'Christmas day gift,' Joe replied matter-of-factly, 'I overheard the guards jeering about it. He's escaped before and they only caught up with him when he decided to make a detour by his favorite weed joint. Can't risk it again, I suppose!' Joe was as tough as they came, and even he did not wish to cross the Kid's path. Before walking through the tall gates, into the compound where he was to spend a considerable part of his life, Joe had been an elite heavy weight pugilist with a number of titles under his belt. A fall from grace occasioned by a nudging knee injury had seen him make the ingress into the murky world of narcotics. He was here to serve time, before they allowed him back for a second shot at boxing stardom. We must have made for an impressive sight, racing away in matching outfits, for a few old timers soon fell in step behind us, perhaps won over by our unwavering commitment. Unwittingly, we had started what would become a formidable running club, but that is a story on its own merits. As the days gave in to months, I found myself disturbed by the fate that awaited Billy the Kid. Yet he carried on, rather nonchalantly, and even seemed grateful for the increased rations from the guards. Of course, I could see through the charade, but I had no means of communicating to Billy, who had been recently moved to solitary confinement. I admit to feeling sorry for him, even hoping that he would escape, which was all too strange, given that I did not really know him. On Christmas day, Joe and I watched as two guards approached Solitary and emerged leading a strapped Billy down the corridor and behind the block. Billy's crew watched from a distance, and the air was charged with suspense. Resuming our Run, we were only too eager to leave it all behind. What happened next was inexplicable! For what sounded like a melee of sorts ensued from behind the Solitary block. Out of it emerged Billy the kid, free of his harness, flanked on either side by two accomplices, and making a run for it. Without warning, they seemed to change direction.

'They are coming our way!' Joe shouted, his heavy breathing smothering the words. Ahead of us, the ground was bare, with no hiding place in sight. At their present pace, it would only be moments before Billy and his gang were upon us! 'Keep running,' Joe admonished, before a  loud guttural sound from Billy stopped us dead in our tracks! I stood mesmerized, as Billy came up to me and our eyes locked! No words transpired between us during that brief encounter and with a slight bow of his fabled head, Billy rejoined his friends, and vanished into the dense shrubbery that lined the far side of the yard. Joe remained speechless.

The Sports club did not slaughter Billy the goat that Christmas. And I was to see him severally over the next couple of months, browsing peacefully with the rest of the tribe. Soon the Club was to change hands and in his acceptance speech, the new owner extolled the virtues of regular exercise and a healthy diet. He urged all to embrace the vegan way of life as he himself had, and decreed that animal products would no longer feature on the Club's menu. Joe walked out of the gates that Christmas, never to return. He went on to become a contender for the heavyweight belt.

I wish him nothing but the best

# THE START

What better place to start than at the beginning? The human body is quite the perfect invention, capable of the most amazing feats. Without letting the cat out of the bag, I can tell you that I train twice a day, six days a week, pushing the limits in the gym, track and across rugged trails. Diversity is my stronghold, and my coach is a big proponent of interval training and reverse-splits. My Achilles heel is the meal, but my dogged dietician is bent on having her way. Sunday is my rest day and I get to sleep in and act normal. This is my life! I have spent countless hours practising for the Start. The first thing you want to do is relax. You relax by taking deep measured breaths. You relax by focusing on the finish. The battle is re-enacted on the track, but it is won or lost during practice. You practise so much, it becomes second nature. You split the intervals into slices, until your reflexes can tell apart a milli- from a micro-second; a nano from a pico - because by the time you set foot upon that track, learned instinct takes over and it's autopilot all the way. There is applause as your name is announced and your image is splurged across the big screen. All these register subliminally, for the moment you enter the arena, man relinquishes control to Machine. And after all gladiators are accorded due respect, you take your place at the start of lane three. "On your marks!" a voice shatters the fabric of night and a palpable hush descends upon the flood lit spectator stands. You give your legs a final stretch before fitting each on to its pedal. A virtual synapse connects foot to lever. Lightning fast reaction times are of essence. The front pedal on which your power foot rests is set two foot lengths from the starting line, the back pedal at three. You prefer the high block even as Michael Johnson favoured the short block for his world breaking 19.32 over the 200 back in '96. Your hands fall in position, shoulder width apart, and just about 2 inches away. You stare down the track at the finish line. You relax by taking deep measured breaths. "Set!" the voice commands, and as your quick-side knee eases off the front pedal, you feel the tension build up in your fast twitch muscle fibres. The set hold should last 2 to 3 seconds, but the rules of physics break down here. Your hips jut out just beyond your shoulder line, and you instinctively tuck in your middle. Your head stays low and completes a smooth curve with your neck and spine. The first decibels are picked up by alert sensors fractions of a second before the sound of the starter gun reverberates across the entire Olympic stadium. Your lungs exhale forcefully, and your feet push off with tremendous force. Your arms pull against the rush of air, as your quick-side leg bolts into full extension. You keep your head low, as you accelerate out of the blocks... I have spent countless hours practicing for the Start. The first thing you want to do is relax. You relax by taking deep measured breaths. You relax by focusing on the finish. Because by the time you set foot upon that track, learned instinct takes over, and it's autopilot all the way. And in that historic race that felled the World Record, all these elements combined superbly, executing flawlessly. On the gigantic screen, in the wake of the race, when they cast the re-run in slow motion, I watched as the first ten meters of Tartan unraveled beneath my feet in well under two seconds and the next ten in just about a second – so that by the sixty metre mark, the clock recorded a top speed of 27.8 miles per hour, fluctuating only slightly when the finish tape was breached. The world could be forgiven for attributing my beaming smile to the sheer exhilaration of the win.

I can tell you now, without revealing too much, that the World Record tumbled on a Saturday night, and on Sunday, I get to sleep in and act normal.

That is my life.

# THE CHAMPION

It never occurred to me to write about my friend, despite the fact that I am credited with several articles in the local daily, mostly reviews on the dismal state of the health care system. But I must add that they are not too bad either, as many an occasion has my editorial prowess secured a drink or two at the local watering hole. However, I subscribe to the unpopular notion that a writer should write to fill a void in knowledge and not merely encumber the shelf with yet another release that would unduly cause a tree to forfeit its life; for what is there to write about an enigmatic personality regarded the greatest marathon runner of all time, that has not been put down before and by the most eminent of scribes? Furthermore, would the opinion of a rural doctor, supplementing a meagre wage through a few third rate articles in the local daily, attract the reader's perusal, let alone tickle the publisher's fancy? Seems like yesterday, when we would scurry all over the countryside, in tattered garb and bare feet, our dilapidated books crumbling away in the morning breeze so that we could only stare in despair as our homework, scribbled painstakingly under the hostile glare of a tin lamp, fluttered away in the wake of the morning draught - to the peril of our much troubled bottoms. And even then, my friend would easily outrun the gasping pack, dashing past the school gate just in time to escape the school master's dragnet. And though his grades were nothing to write home about, he was invaluable in the field, and it was a pleasure to watch from the safety of the spectator stands as the rival outfit chased after him, invariably in utter futility, at those annual inter-school fixtures. We often hunted, not big game of course, but the forest at the edge of the village did boast some mean creatures like wild hares, moles and the much dreaded warthog. We children would chase after the smallest of bucks only to retreat even faster when the cornered animal turned to face its pursuers. And as expected, my friend always emerged the victor, whichever direction we deemed fit to take under the prevailing circumstances. We never thought it would end, the frivolous life with all its trappings, but inevitably age was to catch up with us and we soon went our different ways and to our dissimilar destinies. 'Once we moved like the wind' a quote attributed to the American Indian leader Geronimo, instantly became his most cherished, when we had outgrown our village backyard and were now eager students of World History at the provincial secondary school. Memorable days those, when my friend, quite effortlessly I might add, relegated to the annals of athletics all the standing records in the middle and long distance races. It seemed only a matter of time before he stamped his authority on the world stage. He used to say that running gave him a release from the drudgery of normal life.

'Almost like when you raise your scalpel,' he once told me, and only much later on, did I truly understand the quirky analogy.

When he defended his title at the Boston Marathon, last year, he ran like the Champion he always was. I stood cheering along the home stretch as his lone silhouette emerged round the last bend. And for a moment, a split second etched in eternity, he seemed to move like Geronimo's wind.

And as the world crowned him Champion, I saw us, little children, scurrying across the countryside, fearful for our much troubled bottoms.